Eden Underground

Alessandro Manzetti

English Editing:
Jodi Renée Lester

Proofread by:
Jacqui Corn-Uys and Paula Limbaugh

Crystal Lake Publishing
www.CrystalLakePub.com
(receive a free eBook by joining our newsletter)

Copyright Acknowledgements

"The Monkey with the Big Head" has been previously published in the Spring 2015 issue of The Horror Zine Magazine. "Interiora II" has been previously published in the second edition of the collection *The Shaman and Other Shadows*. "Green Apples" will appear in the June issue of the Disturbed Digest.

Table of contents

The Last Prey

Eva has a snake tattooed on her arm
and a blue orchid in her hair;
fossil ovaries
are carved on the buckle
of her chain mail belt;
her hands are full of blood.
I'm hiding in the tall grass,
grey as the sky,
as the rats show me the way
to escape.

I'm the last man
in this heretic Eden, in this game preserve.
I'm just a flesh trophy,
an aquarium of dried, floating sperm,
poisoned by a powerful pesticide.

I crawl like a worm.
I hear Eva's steps
trampling my trail,
her hallucinated chants;
the smell of female and nightmare
spread all around,
dripping on dry branches.

There is no horizon
to reach.
The land is endless.
A rustle behind me,
then in front, left and right.
I'm fucked, surrounded.
I stand up unsteadily.
I give myself to the cloned Amazons,
to the many copies of Eva,
singing as sirens without a sea,
rubbing male skulls on their thighs.

The Monkey with the Big Head

The man with the big head
crosses the gate of the asylum.
He leaves behind himself the smell of iron,
the rough sheets and the fleas' claws,
the walls of his too-white room
scrawled with numbers, broken lines,
roads dangling from the ceiling,
small one-eyed faces—
his son nibbled from memory.

The man with the big head
gets on the bus.
There are too many people around,
too many thoughts rustling,
that buzz, those moths—
those black scribbled wings—
who live in his brain,
confuse him.
They make the same noise—
a blender of souls—
of those people crowded,
sweating, looking at his big shoes,
at the round scars on his neck,
counting his bestiality.

Alessandro Manzetti

The garden, the exhausted willows,
pots filled with snail shells,
a bike without chain, the new roof,
his sister, her big boobs,
the nest of a spider in her red hair,
long, tired as the willows,
agonizing on her shoulders,
a crucifix that can't breathe
in that niche of flesh
beneath her goiter.
The man arrived home
smiling, toothless.

The TV is on, blaring.
A pissed preacher
covered in black silk armor
shoots large caliber prayers
with his baptized Kalashnikov.
His sister doesn't smile;
she sits back down in the chair,
her velvet spaceship to heaven,
and whispers to him:
There's something to eat in the fridge.
Get what you want.

The man with the big head
sticks his head inside.
He looks at the lights, the colored packaging,
the bottles of beer and holy water.
He feels the fresh sting on his face,
then the moths resume flapping their wings.
Those flying bastards
have formed a black halo around his head—

Eden Underground

they came from his brain,
out through his mouth, nose, ears.
They want his sister now—
to go into *her* holes.

The man grabs a knife
sunk in an apple pie, a holy cake,
turns off the TV and moves close to his sister,
still hypnotized by the electric preacher—
a noiseless electroshock.
He rips her throat, freeing her from the moths,
from those dark insects that have eaten the brains
of the family Stone for generations.
She will not cross the iron gate
as he did a long time ago, entering Hell
as their son did,
the boy whom everyone called
the monkey with the big head.
The deformed angel
flew away
after the last electric shake.

The man opens his backpack,
pulls out a silver frame—
there is no picture inside.
He puts it on the belly of his sister,
which should always remain empty,
then he leaves the house and
slowly approaches the bus stop.

Pieces of Eden

Many rats live in my Eden,
in this garden full of millions of empty boxes,
of cut cables, of rusty circuits.
The silence roars in my Eden,
while the cries are closed off,
sealed safely in a vault,
hidden with flesh's bullion—
my many Eves torn to pieces.

Her head is in a glass jar.
Her bust is on the table,
painted blue, glossy and glazed.
Her chopped arms and legs
fill an oval copper bathtub—
this is the place where I dive
into her purple marmalade,
where I dream,
where I rise and fall to fish—
at the bottom,
the black pearls of my madness.

My Eden is an old abandoned warehouse
between the crooked streets of the suburbs
where ghost cars are parked,
where I drag each new Eve,
still in one piece.

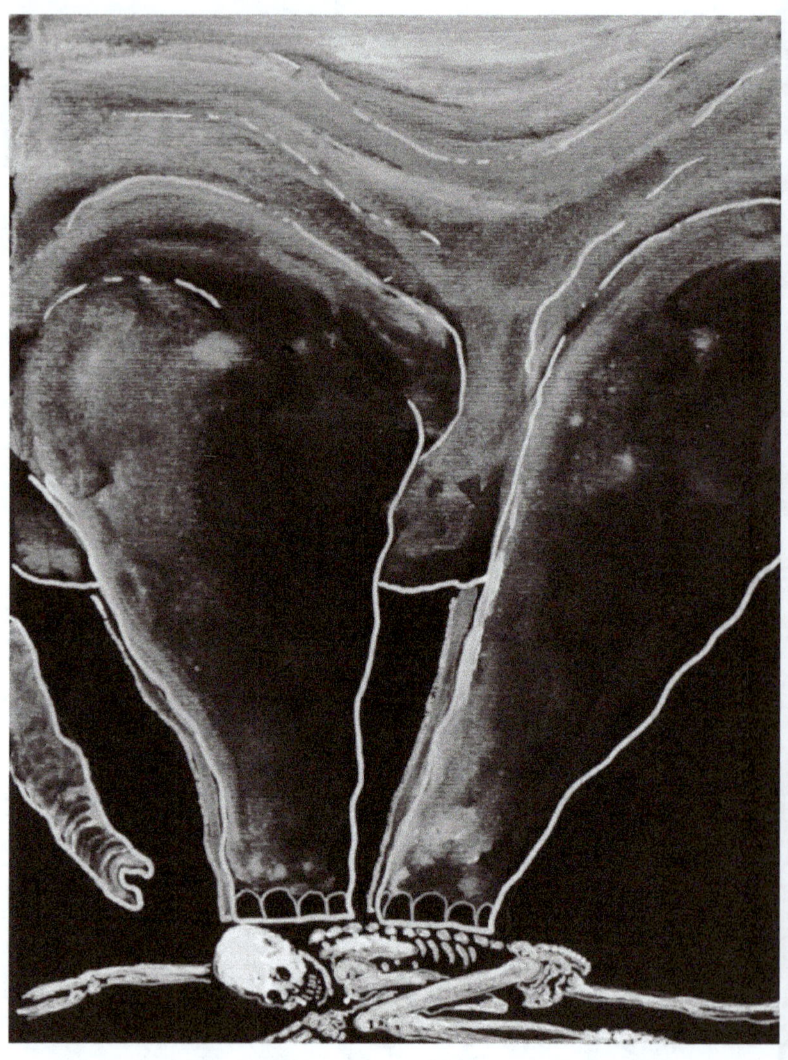

The Dead Circus

Around the circus,
the ground is black.
There is no life for miles.

The tiger without a tail, without teeth,
growls at the shadows
that lick its nose.
It has a lock around its neck
and a ghost as a master.

The fat lady
exploded two years ago,
eating her husband
and the bronze diamonds
of her stage python,
its radioactive skin
green, like the mud from the Apocalypse
fucking the city.

The dwarf, the tightrope walker,
who has never been afraid of anything,
married a young sow
and now goes to the slaughterhouse every morning
with his sons still alive on a leash.

The owner of the circus,
the great Hector,
the magician who could make
the faces of the audience
and their wallets disappear,
now continues to dig,
finding pieces of his daughter
trampled by the elephant's feet
beneath the dirt of the center ring.

The bearded lady
is chained
to her throne of thorns.
At her feet is a long line
of petrified lovers,
carved from the curse of Medusa
by the acid rain of the Apocalypse
frying everything.

The knife thrower, Modì,
still wears his mask of death.
He is the only one to continue the show.
Ghosts applaud from the stands
while he launches his blades
toward the wooden wheel that spins,
empty, without its flesh target.
That squeaky wheel is the only noise
of the dead circus,
of that show you bought the ticket for
when you were born.

Green Apples

Juanita wobbles on her heels, earrings shaking like
rattles,
fifteen years old,
fifteen customers a day,
a father swallowed by the couch,
and a mother, a hooker like her,
chewed up two years ago
in the village of worms
underground.

"Juanita!"
He wants his cold beer.
"Juanita, holy shit!"
He wants to celebrate his gods
with steel helmets and numbers on their chests.
"Juanita, I'll kill you one of these days!"
The screen turns on to the Super Bowl.
The temple is open,
but the customer honks.
—Fuck!—
Juanita must hurry.
She has to open the fridge,
and then her skinny legs.
The pig in the suit waits for her,
out there in his sticky car.

Alessandro Manzetti

Stories of skinned knees,
curses, and drool
dripping down her back;
stories of Sundays in a January
of quarterbacks and crumpled dollars
tucked into her panties—
green, soft bullets
planted in the depths of the soul.
Juanita runs down the stairs.
She stops on the first floor
and sticks two green apples into her empty bra.
Now she's ready.

"Juanita!"
The father starts to yell.
He finished his beer, again.
His empty green bottle roars.
He hates his skinny boy,
without real tits,
who earns a third as much as the mother.
—Fuck!—
He spits another day on the carpet.
"I'll have to go back to work,
sooner or later."

Juanita opens the car door.
She smells of fresh fruit,
unripe, peeled,
cut into thin slices.
"Ten dollars."
Love can be so green.

Koo-o

The cage is on the beach.
Koo-o raises his scepter of bones.
All the others kneel,
while the neck of a blue parrot
twists right and left,
toward the ocean that touches on
the edges of the new cemetery,
the plantation of burnt human heads
emerging from the sand.

The plane sank into the ocean long ago.
Grey morays live in its iron armor,
darting through the windows
with purple eyes
and pieces of men between their teeth.
The survivors had reached the island,
wading through its algae guts,
coming up against the white eyes
of Koo-o and his clan.

The man in the cage
has a long beard
and two parrot wings tattooed on his back,
carved by a shard of stone—
wings that bleed again—
above a nest of deadwoods.
Koo-o orders the others

to bring the torches,
to inflame the body of the man
who can't shout his thoughts,
who can't hear the drums of death;
his tongue, his ears
have become trophies
hanging on Koo-o's necklace.

Survivors fallen from heaven
were welcomed to the island,
like angels, like divine birds.
Koo-o and his tribe
wanted to see them fly again
from the rock towers at the top.
They wanted to learn, to discover the secrets
of the people who live between the clouds,
still able to see the sun
hidden from the eternal eclipse
of the radioactive dust
of the Apocalypse.

The man in the cage burns.
Koo-o approaches the bars,
smells the acrid stink of cooked flesh,
motioning for the others to approach
to see how a fake angel dies,
just like all the other gods
who can't fly anymore,
buried on the beach.
Koo-o is the emperor of the island,
of the latest Eden,
with his crown of blue parrot feathers,
with his dead necklaces.

Eden Underground

He will pierce the clouds,
the green siege of the Apocalypse.
He'll discover the secrets of the sky
and teach all the other gorillas
now that he has learned how to kill,
how to burn angels,
to enjoy and rave
between the black thighs of Death,
the queen of the murderers.

Interiora II

Lightning. The sky is pissed.
The suburb of Rome
is an appetizer of the Purgatory
you can see on the high tide of asphalt,
broken bones, corpses of sirens,
fish bones, and remains of oceans.
It's raining. A dog limps
toward the tent of an abandoned circus,
looking for its master—
a clown without a head or a smile—
with dust on his tongue
and black grease on his rump.

Venus is sleeping
in the yellow building.
She's polluted, as are her dirty sheets.
Her flesh is gone.
Ribs and bones triumph,
waiting for someone else adrift
on her solitary raft,
floating on the edge of reality.

Two hundred dollars for a whole night
with her, with Venus,
with her remains.
Then comes the morning light—

Eden Underground

so sharp—
along with the roar of a mower.
The client wakes up
and opens the window.
The stink of gasoline and sadness
enters the room.

He looks out
toward the cemetery of cars
waiting for souls, drivers.
Venus is still in bed.
She's without armor now.
Her teeth sparkle,
showing a skeleton smile.
Her flesh is gone,
along with the subway of her uterus,
the generous glands,
the Byzantine back, and the skin of a mango—
all that she was yesterday.

"Where is my Venus?"
thinks the man leaning against the wall,
eyes popping out of his head.
He tries to break down the door
to get away from that velvet-tongued monster.

Two hundred dollars for a night
with Venus' sister
(Death? Life?),
for her black ring and white bones,
for that damned room,
close, immense,
sealed by an old welder.

Alessandro Manzetti

The subway swallows its passenger.
All the church bells ring together,
making the ears of the dog prick up,
holding one of its master's bones
in its rotten teeth.

Eastern Heaven

Heaven is overbooked.
There is no place for anyone else.
Outside is a great borderless Hell—
above ground, underground,
there is no difference.
A trident made of stone
rises among the peaks of the Himalayas,
a tail jutting out from the
sulphurous ass of the world.

Heaven is now protected by a wall,
by cement guard towers,
by checkpoints and loaded machine guns.
Off Limits
If you die—
and one day you will—
and the mollusc of your white pearl soul
tries to crawl to the entrance
and pass the red line,
the guards won't think twice about shooting you.
Everyone will see through
your new holes.

Angels trained as snipers.
Saints with white beards and shiny halos,
the insignia of generals sewn on their epaulets.

You must have an organized army
to protect the new Heaven.
Daily, thousands of souls and molluscs,
thousands of slimy paws emerging from soft bodies,
their own shells buried somewhere.

They call it Eastern Heaven,
this new Heaven,
that place surrounded by a large wall,
covered with graffiti and phosphorescent urine,
the spattered colors of souls left out.
You can see the whites, the blues,
of their mortal imagination.
The old Heaven,
the one with ancient paintings and
gothic cathedral windows;
the one populated by cherubs and archangels with eyes
on their wings;
the one full of clouds, full of silence.
The one without the traffic of teeth—
outside, off the wall—
of giant barracudas,
with their bloody silver-scaled skin,
wallowing in that ocean of Hell.
The same predators who nip at human flesh
in real life, for a lifetime.
The same monsters, with jaws much larger,
are here
in this expanded Hell.

Red Monsoon

To Aisha

Chiku is thirteen.
Her hair is full of knots and sand,
a gift from the Kismayo monsoon,
carrying everywhere
the crumbs of the Indian Ocean
abandoned on a large elliptical bay.
Chiku has big eyes,
lined up with the equator, accustomed to large spaces,
but now they are in the darkness
covered by a black cloth.
Chiku is a whore now, for the law,
raped by three camouflaged soldiers,
Somali wolves with helmets.
Herds of anger that never sleep.

The stadium is packed.
Chiku is the main attraction,
buried in the ground, only her head exposed.
The executioners are ready to strike,
to cut off her signal,
slowly.
A truck roars, raises its green back,
and dumps out thousands of stones.
Chiku looks at her black equator,
which is now red and hot

after being hit by the first stone,
and her bones crush,
slowly.

The monsoon stops.
It's tired.
It comes from Mogadishu;
sits in the stands of the stadium
and cries for Chiku,
ignoring the applause of the wolves
and their adrenaline kettledrums.
The monsoon becomes small, narrow,
and it runs into the girl's mouth,
still alive.
Chiku swells, more and more,
and then explodes.

The executioners are disappointed.
They remove the pieces of her
from their faces, from their arms;
they mumble, blaspheme.
The little whore
who denounced three wolves
has not suffered enough . . .
The monsoon, now free,
takes a deep breath and, with invisible nails,
sweeps everything away,
tearing black-tongued spectators
and bodies in uniform.

The equator is tinged with red.
This time it's true;
only the stones and the wolves' teeth remain,
scattered over an empty hole in the ground.

A Modern Berserker

Even here—at the checkpoint,
waiting for a bastard
stuffed with bombs
under the cursed sun of this city of sand.
"Jack died yesterday."
His head landed on the hood
of the armored truck,
bouncing on the American flag,
faded.

Still here, waiting for the tricks of Death,
hiding beneath old rags,
in children's eyes,
inside baskets of dates fallen from the palms of Babylon.
Matt is busy on the radio.
It's time to sniff my white poison,
my Eden powder.
Yeah, now I feel good,
as strong as a bear ready to fuck Death
and all its invisible creatures, big and small,
appearing from nowhere,
with C4 clenched in their damned teeth.

A woman on a bike stops nearby.
She smiles.
Her fingers are painted purple.
She wears a black robe, a veil on her head;

you can only see the eyes, two oil wells,
through the slits of a golden mask
that covers the nose and mouth.
She looks like a ghost.

The bitch approaches Matt.
My bear blood boils.
I jump down and take her by the neck.
I'm drooling, and the sand comes up in my brain.
I take the knife from my belt to open her belly
and let her give birth to the bomb.

Matt cries—he pushes me away—
I fall to the ground and stare at the yellow sky.
My companion doesn't know that I am a bear now,
one of those you can't fool.
I get up, I feel like a god, I'm his fate.
The hairs on my back stand on end,
my paws raise up,
and I stick my blade into his forehead;
all this happens in seconds.
He looks at me, surprised.
"Why?"
While Death pulls down his pants.
"Why?"

My ghost gets back on the bicycle.
She smiles again
and then disappears.

The Half Bride

Cold flesh
hanging with diamond cuffs
on asphalt veins,
capturing headlights, metal sheets,
rushed and braked eyes.
Winter skin is on show
on the road for free,
under the feet of the pines,
under their latex roots,
arching their backs
everywhere,
like white-blood alien snakes.

The half bride
lives behind the last curve.
Her dress is alive,
sewn from hundreds of pairs of wings
of motionless violet black moths,
You can strip her simply by blowing.
She'll guide you to her plastic altar.
A priest will emerge from the ground,
his head breaking
the winter garden, your Eden,
covered with snails and tin crucifixes.

Alessandro Manzetti

"Are you sure you want her?"
Her golden hair jellyfish
is already between your legs,
clinging to your skin,
injecting
poisonous clouds and Venus' proteins into your mind.
Now you will see with three eyes.
It moves up and down,
stretching its tentacles,
leaving you to drown
in the ocean of sweat in your used car.
It's too late to say no
to her siren tongue.
"Yes, I'm sure."

The rotten priest smiles at you;
the wedding is going to be celebrated.
A pink butterfly
with yellow, radioactive skulls on the wings
comes out of his mouth
along with his blessing.
The ground regains its priest,
swallowing him with all the magic caterpillars
growing in his stomach.

The half bride
spits something out of her mouth
and shoves a black ring on your finger,
a ring which burns.
You resist, thinking of the ice,
the North Pole, your wife's limbo.
Hit by a truck, two years ago.
You dig in your smashed pockets

Eden Underground

finding a holy card
and fifty dollars.
They are hers now.
You come home on foot,
no money for gas,
no bride by your side.

Eden Underground

The man continues to dig.
His hands are blistered
and the shovel is too small.
A crow watches him, shaking its head,
drawing straight lines in the air
with its sharpened beak.
The bird tears a feather from its chest,
which falls, slowly, onto the shiny skull of the man
who continues to dig.

The hole, wide and deep,
swallows the man up to the neck;
that place is not a cemetery.
The man pierces the skin of his garden.
Green blood splashes out,
the shovel's iron tongue
cuts the veins of the roots—
bowels with head and tail—
What is the man looking for?

Finally the ground reveals
what it has in its belly—
continually trampled—
a carcass covered with white fur.
It shows itself, again, in the eyes of the master,
deflated, held together
by a frame of ribs.

Eden Underground

The lungs are full of moths,
underground wings and nests;
they're breathing instead of the animal.
The man crouches next to his dead dog,
barking, growling,
spitting out his humanity,
drooling turbid, poisoned memories.

The bitch that left him;
the factory dismantled, closed,
the metal powder still under his fingernails;
the soft fat of indifference;
the python of unemployment around his neck
which, like a bastard brown and yellow tie,
tightens, getting stronger;
his overdue fifty years,
the ghost that continues to mutter, "Too late!";
his mother, a wobbly pudding
without muscles, bones, thoughts,
following the routes of her madness
aboard a flying wheelchair
driven by a Romanian Amazon.

The man looks at the sky for the last time.
He has a dry throat now.
He stands up in the middle of the pit,
pushing in mounds of soil from the edge above him,
over his sleeping dog
whom he had called Eden,
the only creature among many useless bipeds
that had never stopped believing in him:
its hero with thousands of pockets,
its god with a sad smile.

Carlos, Diego, Vamos!

Fat red-faced gravediggers
feel their hands burning
when the ropes run between their fingers.
The coffin is lowered into the pit.
Mr. Time, with his blue beard,
throws a handful of earth
in that model abyss.
Nobody believes what happened.
"How can Death die?"
"And now, what do we do?"

Mrs. AIDS pretends to cry,
takes a handkerchief
from her crocodile skin purse.
She blows her nose, hiding a smile.
She had always hated that fat bitch,
her too-demanding employer,
her thick neck, encircled by fake pearls
wide as the mouth of a volcano.

Mr. Plague, almost extinct—
nobody recognizes him—
makes the sign of the cross
while his wide-brimmed hat
crumbles.

Mrs. War acts as the first lady, as usual.
She wears grenade jewels,
her long hair in a bun
held together by two bayonets.
Her red lips seem to whisper—
count—
the souls ready for the napalm.
"Where will her children end up now?"
"The bitch has left a will?"
"Where are the fucking keys to the warehouse of
elsewhere?"
From the trunk of a cypress
a human face sticks out.
Curious.
No, it's Maria. You can recognize
her two-tailed mermaid tattoo,
the mark on her neck
engraved by her first pimp—
copyright Iceman Charlie.
The woman laughs.
She enjoys the scene.
She killed them—
Death and Cancer married one year ago—
their throats slashed.

The funeral is over.
Maria calls her two children—
"Carlos, Diego, *vamos!*"—
to go back to the Spanish district.
She did it for them: seven and eleven years old.
She learned as a child
to use the night,
to use the knife,

Eden Underground

to cut throats and testicles
of pimps and too-demanding bosses.
"Carlos, Diego, vamos!"

The Wrath Sings, Goddess

The chariot of Achilles,
dragged by two big rats,
dashes around the walls of Troy,
the trail of Hector's blood
drawing three concentric circles.

A strige with the beak of a crow
sucks the blood,
the red shapes of Hector,
waving its purple feathers.
Hecuba, from her high tower,
shows her bare breasts,
squeezing them between her fingers;
a drop of milk—
the first milk of Hector—
drops on the sand,
exploding like a meteorite.

Death emerges from that crater,
wearing the Achaean armor,
the leather helmet inlaid with boar tusks
and a crest of black horsehair.
He strips the gold and silver plates
from his chest, pulling out
three deflated, dried out breasts,
his sharp bronze nipples,

Eden Underground

and shouts:
"You'll have to drink it, sooner or later!"
He throws a spear against the sky,
piercing it, exposing
the other side of the blue leather
of that imaginary canopy;
now you can see the plasma of the endless night,
the black salt of the world,
and thousands of chariots, rats, warriors, and heroes
passing by quickly,
dragging corpses with long leather strings.

Achilles continues his mad dash;
then, at the end of the third lap,
drives his rats and Hector's corpse
into that black hole, taking a running start
on the oblique horizon,
accelerating.
The chariot soars,
penetrating that illusion of black butter
in the fourth circle drawn today
on the sand of Troy.

The hole closes,
crushing winners and losers.
It turns into a porthole, one of many along the side
of a flying submarine—
the night with engines and propellers—
from which Death can enjoy the madness of war,
moving from one century to another,
pushing endless buttons,
sniffing guts of selfishness—
still alive—

animated by a mysterious power,
like recently severed lizards' tails.

The Rime of the Mad Mariner

Part I

A hand, a frozen claw,
grabs the blue coat of the bride's brother.
The man turns,
his shape sinks into the foolish eyes of the Mariner,
who smells of digested beer, rusty thoughts,
barnacles encrusted on the bow
which cuts Hell's waterway in two.
"What are you doing here, beggar?"

The bridegroom's doors are opened wide.
The wedding dress has a long tail—
white—
the same color of the dust
that fries the brain of the bride's brother
who observes the scene
and the new beauty of his sister.
He spits on the ground, trying to shake his anxiety.
White blood galloping in him,
neighing and drooling.
The party is starting; the guests are waiting for him.
"Keep off, you fucking drunk!"

But the eyes of the Mad Mariner
are sparkling, invisible hooks
that drag both flesh and soul

wherever they want.
The man stands still,
listens like a three-year-old child.
His muscles become granite
while everything around him moves fast;
a circle of fat moths
that don't give a damn about the sun.
The morning,
which makes the worms sleep,
forms around his head.
The Mariner hath his will.
Charon loosens the moorings.

"There was a ship"—
The Mariner begins to tell—
"which cleared the harbor,
making its way between the thighs of the sea,
its mast
strong, imposing, excited;
its propellers
stuffed with chopped sirens . . . "

The bride, her dress
sewn with generous lines,
paces in the hall.
Between scarlet glances,
the wedding guests
sniff the extinct smell of virginity,
the ghost that was not invited—
there will be no blood on the sheets tonight—
The man can't join the others,
yet he can't choose but to hear
the hoarse voice of the Mad Mariner

Eden Underground

bellowing in his empty cave,
in his slippery life, in his prison.
He's trapped behind the bars of
poisonous cocaine stalactites,
harder than steel.

" . . . and suddenly the storm blast came,
and it was blind and deaf, tyrannical,
like the kicks of a pissed off god
with thirty-yard feet.
The ship drove fast,
creaking and moaning,
and southward we fled.
Then that motherfucking god
guided us into his bladder,
full of ice blocks
that floated around like huge emeralds;
a virtual necklace surrounded us—
the necklace of a madam descending a staircase
to take care of her customers;
Death, cold and lonely,
with her chest full of jewels
and pockets filled with skulls
that can no longer see.

"Not shapes of men or of beasts,
only fog-formed illusions seemed alive.
Black clouds with sharp teeth
opened their wide mouths, their jaws unhinged.
Spinal columns emerged from the sea
without skin or flesh,
bony snakes of what had been."

The bride's brother
listened to the story, unmoving.
His nose dripped—
white—
like the keel of the ship.
The cursed ship of the Mad Mariner.
A stain on his pants, between his legs,
grew steadily; even that was white.
The garden had disappeared.
The sounds of the party are swallowed,
like everything else,
by a giant toad
sitting on the edge of the man's mind,
ready to jump and take it all away.

"At last a blessing was among us;
a girl came through the fog.
She was a ray in that ice graveyard.
She ate what we gave her,
what the storm had left to us—
beans, dried meat—
She was hungry.

"The ice did split with a thunder fit;
the helmsman steered us through.
We were free!
But the girl was not a siren with shark teeth.
She had long legs, long bones, no tail;
but she wasn't an angel.
She was beautiful, an alien sunflower
that turns toward too many stars,
making them slaves
of her small crown of yellow spears,

Eden Underground

of her rough pubescence
oozing Saturn's honey.
Her floral axis, its roots dug into the wooden planks,
became the totem, the altar, of my companions.

"I realized after nine nights
that the chains of storm, of fate, were better
than those of that demon
with amber skin and white fingers;
a strange Venus born of an ice womb
in extreme solitude,
which makes it all the same at first glance:
men, seagulls, whales, beans—
living things, big or small,
to play with, and then to cut into pieces,
inside and out,
with the blade of boredom."

"God save thee, old fool
from your madness!"
the bride's brother screams,
his tongue finally loose,
swallowing nails
in his bitter, drugged throat.
But the Mariner doesn't give up his prey.
He must tell the end of his story
before leaving.
"With my knife . . . I kill the girl,"
he continued.

Part II

"It was too late to kill her.
The girl had already given birth,
her white, slimy eggs on the deck
filled with other girls that throbbed
in their web of veins.
On board there was the plague of demons—
I was the only one to see them.
My companions hated me
for killing the big sunflower, the mother
of those beautiful creatures
that came out of their shells.

"They copulated, screaming like pigs,
the grip of those white virgin thighs
breaking backs and souls.
I saw it, floating in the cold sea,
where they had thrown me
after tying my neck with the guts of an albatross,
because, they said,
I'll never fly like that dismembered bird.
I had to pay for my crime—
Killer of sunflowers!

"Night came on the scene
wearing its more obscene dress,
its black lips and red tongue
covered with incandescent corals.
While the current pushed me toward the banks
of the ship, in the distance

Eden Underground

I saw dancing wildfires and sperm rainbows.
The water, like a witch's oils,
burned green and blue.
Then the sea became completely white,
and on the shore where I sat and waited,
the bloated corpses of my companions
began arriving,
a neat row of black stuff
in that huge white sea."

"Let me go, you're crazy!"
The bride's brother
bit his lips until they bled
to escape the illusions
of the cursed Mariner.
He closed his eyes, the vision vanished.
He found himself in front of the mirror,
the old fool was crumbled—
white powder, two strips
on top of the sink—
The brother takes his credit card,
divides the two parallel lines, and sniffs deeply.
"Wow, fuck those stories!"
The shape of a ship appears in the mirror.
"Damn!"
The brother looks at the scene
through a deformed porthole:
Two women playing dice in the cabin. They laugh.
Their skin, troubled by leprosy, goes to pieces.
The game is done! I've won! I've won!
Quoth she and whistles thrice.
They laugh, they speak loudly.

The brother looked upon the rotting deck,
and there lay the dead men—
the companions of the old fool—
their eyes open,
looking through the same porthole
to the other side:
they observe the bride's brother,
his face too white, his invisible chain
heavier than the guts of albatrosses
around the neck of the Mad Mariner.
They know he is going to die.
They expect to take him across
to the other side.
The brother falls to the ground,
hidden memories bouncing out:

—His sister, wedding dress on the bed—
—Her right breast sneaking out of the bra—
—The dogs of cocaine, out of their cage, growling—
—The sex viper biting, snapping forward—
—Leprosy liquid gushing—
—The rape, his bleeding knuckles—
—Keep your mouth shut, or I'll kill you!—

The guests rush,
shouting in dismay.
The Mad Mariner moves away;
there is too much confusion.
Death has wasted its time.
It was useless to try to convince the man
that its proposal was better than the death of life
offered by his sister, the blonde bitch
who had won the man's soul at dice.

Eden Underground

She takes off the old skin
and combs her long, black hair.
She grabs a glass of champagne.
The party is not over yet.

The bride kneels before the body of her brother.
She sees foam dangling from his mouth—
heart attack—
You deserve it, you bastard!
But white eggs are growing in her belly,
slimy, fresh eggs.
Death in life doesn't like to lose a game.
It's better to start over
with the son of the bastard—
nine months will pass quickly.

But soon he heard the splash of oars,
He heard the pilot's cheer;
His head was turned perforce away
And he saw a boat appear.

(Inspired by Samuel Taylor Coleridge's *The Rime of the Ancient Mariner*.)

Lacrimosa

The girl cries,
sitting on her piece of sidewalk.
The ravens dance, cawing,
forming a narrow, black circle
around the little hooker
who plugs her ears not to hear.
Their beaks suck
at the puddles of tears,
small oceans from young eyes,
without a seabed,
without coral's colorful bones.

The biggest raven observes the scene,
keeping its balance on a branch—
the totem of flesh that everyone venerates—
it flaps its wings,
its chorus of feathers
merged with the strident violins
of the car's brakes,
singing for the girl
below the streams of her runny makeup.
The girl's face is streaked by black lines,
infinite.
They are her faded thoughts, watered down,
drawing the lines of a requiem,
a white pentagram
on a black background.

Eden Underground

The first customer of the evening
opens the window of his car,
hands a handkerchief to the girl,
then his sticky tongue,
the one of a heretic chameleon,
snaps toward his prey,
hitting her lukewarm wings.
The girl is dragged across the asphalt
to the man's mouth,
his reptile heart
and infected belly.

The black car moves away.
The biggest raven chases it
toward the parking lot to the east,
a graveyard of strains, beheaded trees;
a rectangle of cement
pierced by gold manholes
which lead straight to hell.

The bird rotates its turbid eyes,
sees the man sucking his fingers,
enjoying,
pants down,
the taste of honey and Eden's tomatoes,
the bittersweet, delicious pulp
of the torn, sold adolescence,
licking as the god of the saddest violins—
salt, tides, tears
of a sea never crossed
never pierced by a bow.
Amen.

The Pawn Shop

Temperance runs along the road,
wearing her yellow dress
stained with withered flowers,
rusty petals
fall on the sidewalk,
traces of her
leading to the pawn shop.
Temperance is a broken-hearted woman.
In the pond of her memories,
furious crocodiles are wallowing,
nibbling everything
piece by piece.

Mr. Wang is waiting for her,
as he does every Thursday.
His little eyes scan the windows,
the people passing,
the people who are ashamed to come in.
The wind lifts the tides of petals
from that open-mouthed sidewalk,
a well-known cemetery
full of mousetraps.

Temperance pushes the door,
a bell rings.
Mr. Wang's eyes rotate

Eden Underground

as lemons, cherries, plums,
as the beautiful red sevens
of the slot machines—
all those colorful combinations,
always losers,
diluted by the rotten kidneys of fate.
Dreams of others pissed into the water.
Not those of Mr. Wang
who has a special, shimmering lever—
a sharp scalpel—
that makes him win each time.

Temperance moves the beaded curtain
and enters the back of the shop.
Mr. Wang hangs a red sign on the door:
"I'll be back soon,"
then approaches Temperance,
who is already lying on the table,
the altar of still-good organs,
of spare parts,
the Eden of old rich men,
the new pharaohs
with their assembled bodies,
mosaics of others—
new hearts, new livers,
special discount on a pair of kidneys,
single lung vacuum packed,
each with a label in Chinese
and a price in US dollars.

"What do you sell this time?"
Temperance offers what's left of her still-working flesh:
eyes, uterus . . . heart.

Even if she does not come out alive
without that engine in her chest,
under the faded flowers of the yellow dress,
it might be worth . . .
She can make a lot of money,
enough to pay tuition for her daughter, Mary.
Seventeen years old, blue eyes like headlights.

Mary sells herself whole
on the highway.
Temperance pretends to know nothing about that.
She believes that the lights of airplanes
are real UFOs,
and that the fishnet stockings, the high heels,
the dress that reveals a breast
and has a heart-shaped cutout on the behind
are part of a Halloween costume
that Mary used to wear as a child.
Candy turning into green, sticky dollars.
Halloween every night.

Mr. Wang takes his rate table
and the booklet with customer requests.
"Well," he mumbles.
"The uterus is hard to sell,
especially a thirty-six-year-old one,
but the heart . . . it's as good as gold."
Temperance closes her eyes.
Mr. Wang understands and inserts a rubber tube
into her mouth.
"You will not feel . . . anything.
Just think about diving, slowly,
into the small ocean I'm creating for you."

Eden Underground

The scalpel sinks into Temperance's chest.
The bell on the door rings.
Death moves the beaded curtain,
enters the back of the store,
and sits on an iron stool.
Waiting.

Mary gets in a Mercedes.
A rich client, what luck!
The car leaves, fast as a rocket,
heading toward the woods.
Mary looks at the man, he is young and cute.
He's wearing jeans. They're swelling between the legs.
"What do you like?"
the girl whispers.
The man glances at her blue headlights,
then he slips his hand into his pocket,
moving his knife sideways.
His jeans are tight. That stuff makes him uncomfortable.
He smiles: "I like your eyes."
The car brakes, raising dust.

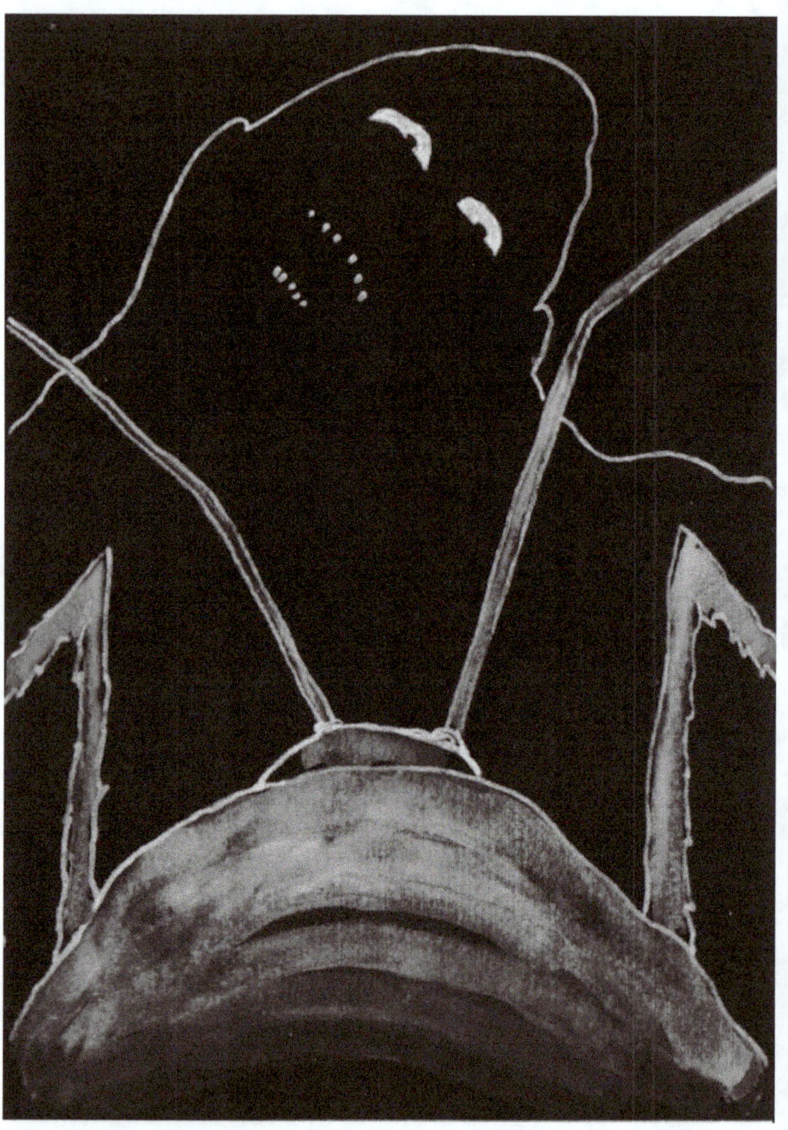

The Cockroach King

Josh doesn't live in the clouds,
he doesn't throw lightning,
he hasn't a long white beard
or an armed escort of angels
with duck wings and loaded Kalashnikovs.
Josh isn't a god.
He's a five-hundred-pound king
surrounded by a court of cockroaches.
His apartment is in Nashville
(where Johnny Cash was born),
Humphreys Street, near Gabby's Burgers and Fries.
It's his Eden, a hunting ground,
his leather armchair in front of the TV,
with a huge bucket of chips on either side.
It's his throne,
his Nirvana with footrest.

The King's cockroaches
are many, are trained,
are smart.
Long lines of insects,
without butler uniforms,
run back and forth
from the kitchen to the living room,
carrying on their joined shells,
as a Roman legion would,
food for the King
who can no longer get up from the armchair.

Alessandro Manzetti

The man mumbles.
A fat cockroach with three antennas,
the team leader, takes the lead of the faster platoon
to bring his monarch
the pot with the boy's stew,
the one who delivered the pizza last night,
delivering even himself,
stuffed with fear, crispy.
The King loves leftovers—
We don't throw away anything in this house!

The row of insects, a living, quivering mosaic, carries on its back
the flaky dish, with the boy's head
already gnawed.
The younger, smaller cockroaches
are behind the group,
pulling two boxes of ketchup.
The floor looks like a great mandala
ready to dissolve at any time:
the dirty, orange carpets,
ruins of slippers and chicken bones,
mayonnaise snakes, salty rattles,
hundreds of cardboard boxes
balanced on the walls
containing large, charred halos of pizza.
Chaos meets Perfection
in the realm of Josh.
Van Gogh couldn't have done it better,
giving life to matter,
transforming colors and flavors.
When the dish finally arrives
on the King's knees,

Eden Underground

someone knocks on the door—
Police! Open it, you bastard!
The cops break down the door,
waving rifles and pistols.
They seem like alien creatures
with their infrared goggles.—
Don't move!
Are you kidding? Josh thinks.
The cockroaches surround their monarch,
forming a perfect circle,
a moat of themselves.
The insects growl, blaspheme,
if you know how to listen.
Josh stretches his arm toward the bucket
to grab a handful of chips,
but the cop with the star on the collar
is nervous and fires two shots.
The bullets pierce the singlet of the King,
getting bogged down in the layer of fat that is
stronger than a bulletproof vest.

The time of the King is over,
the hem is full;
Josh swallows the last chip
and explodes in a hail of flesh—
a real show, better than the gas chamber—
The cop with the star on the collar
grabs the flying head of the boy.
It seems like a cannonball
shot from an old, rotten brig,
adrift.

The Garden

The garden is closer
than you think.
It's not hidden in Mesopotamia
under that big slice of yellow ground
where the Shatt al-Arab melts—
fine sand, water, and angels' piss.

The garden is everywhere,
two blocks from your house
where you pass without knowing it,
riding in your haste.
The garden has only two trees,
many green benches,
a dry fountain with red fish fossils,
and an iron gate, padlocked,
open only on Sundays.

You call it the asylum
because that's what they taught you,
but inside, in the garden,
there are survivors of the Great Flood,
unkempt men and women
wearing white pajamas
walking around a piece of the Ark,
their rotten wood totem.

Eden Underground

The inhabitants of the garden
look around with their hawk eyes,
look out, look at us:
we are their ghosts,
faceless, meaningless.
We are hallucinations with legs and arms
that they have to insult,
to strangle at the earliest opportunity,
before the next shock fries
their memories of Eden.

Dames de Voyage

Flora, my oldest doll,
has latex skin and glass eyes.
She started my Eden,
teaching the craft to the others.
Flora is the favorite
of my inanimate harem.
She always wears the red velvet dress,
the same as Puccini's Floria Tosca,
the same as Callas at the Covent Garden,
with precious trim
along the breast.

Béatrice, who sleeps in bed with me
on Thursdays,
looks like a real woman,
with her silicone flesh,
the articulated joints, and the PVC skeleton.
I love watching her mouth half open,
the rain of her red hair on the pillow.
Béatrice knows how to cry and laugh.
Her artificial sweat
smells of sunflowers.

Doriane, my latest purchase—
$12,000—
is installed on all fours

Eden Underground

in my living room, over the Persian carpet.
She is a custom doll,
a replica of a fat teenager
with slits smaller than those of the others.

Many other dolls live in my Eden,
cold and warm flowers,
eyes fixed on the ceiling
or on the oval windows
from which you can see the roofs of Paris,
the maze and confusion of reality.
Ants running on the roads
are nothing but restless souls,
disordered, shaped by chaos.
But all this shit
remains behind the door,
outside of my Eden.

Wednesday.
It would be Lise's turn.
Her adjustable tits and long fingers,
light and flexible
as the spears of the Macedonian cavalry.
But I can't wait another day
for Béatrice, for her scent of sunflowers—
I change the rules—
The battery is switched on. Her eyes open.
I move her on the bed.
I tighten a leather collar
around her slender white neck.
I push myself between her thighs,
bending her mechanical knees.

Alessandro Manzetti

My back burns, hit by cold flames.
I look back. I see her . . .
Flora wielding a knife,
my blood dripping from her hands.
Above the plastic diamond necklace
appears a wicked smile
that has never been created for her.
Then she pierces her tits,
letting her white love
bleed on the marble floor.

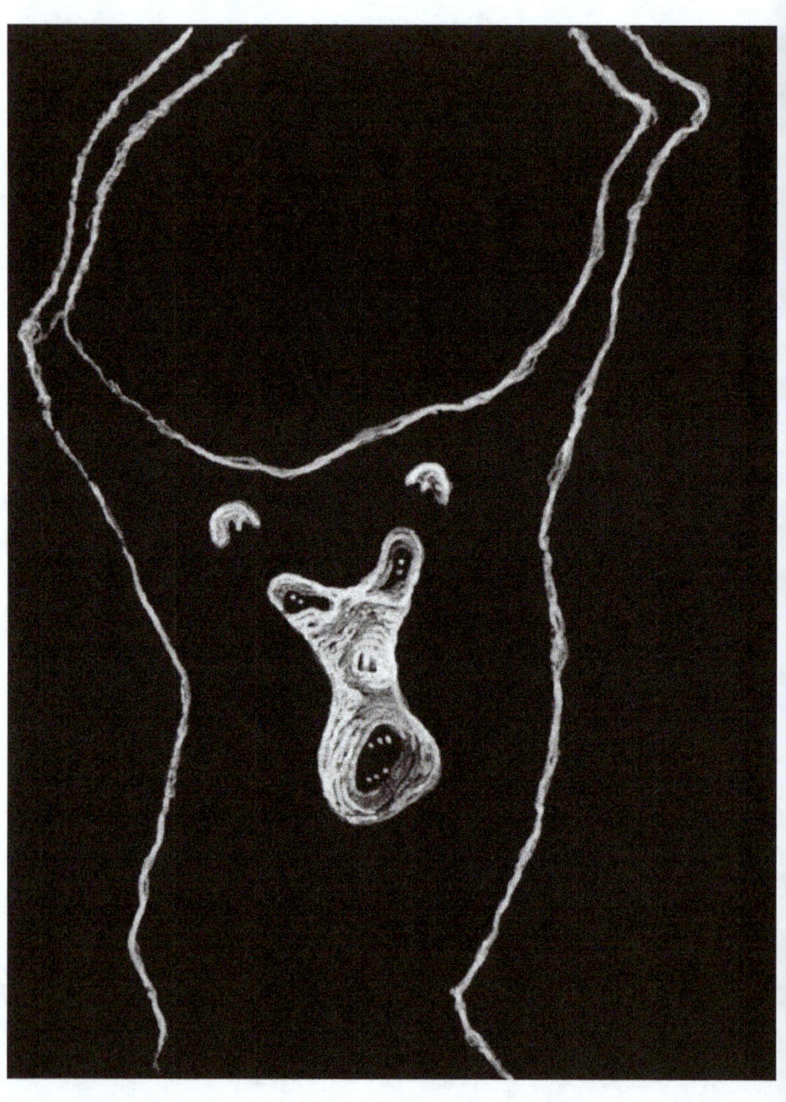

Electric Monkeys

A building scratched by green
phosphorescent moisture;
the laboratory inside,
where shouts are sealed—
The Cage—
A monkey running
inside, with its jaded paws
along the perimeter of a few-inch world,
its steel-bar forest,
where plastic bowls and silicone branches bloom.
The rectangles of stars, their blue neon
always lit—
fake constellations, too many ceilings
inside.

On the right, a companion with its belly open—
ripped—
lying on a table, its tongue out,
surrounded by human butchers
sticking their faces, their lights, into him.
"What are they looking for?"
To the left, the head of its brother
immersed in a plastic tub
with a label full of numbers (4587...)
around its neck.
That head, the monkey knows,

has never been able to swim
or breathe underwater.

The man in the white coat
comes back to The Cage,
holding a magical syringe in one hand,
leather ropes in the other.
The bastard is smiling,
showing perfect white teeth—
the ivory house of his rattlesnake tongue—
while his red-haired friend
drags the electric machine
from which poisonous suckers,
tentacles, and burned monkey hairs
stick out, and upon it
crazy LEDs light up
forming curves of red-dot tides.

Someone turns on the music.
The violas of the first movement
of Mahler's Resurrection
vibrate, languishing for a few seconds,
followed by horns, violins,
and hard-skinned percussions;
all the instruments play together
to overpower the cries
of the electric monkey.

The Tenth Circle

Lucifer, the Beast,
shows the man the rooms of Hell;
the swollen corridors,
the chandeliers made of bone and onyx,
the black bulbs,
screwed cancers,
ten per group,
ten per room.
The metastases of the bottom of the Earth
lit by darkness.

The man looks around,
checks the moisture stains
on the walls.
The basilisks' purple nests
pulse in the corners.
He leans out from the terraces,
from the iron gratings of the windows,
enjoying the view
of the tenth circle attic;
the tallest, the most expensive.

Lucifer stops
in front of a large wall of eyes
that blink open and shut,
forced to constantly watch

the first cascade of the Styx,
the hydrochloric acid river
that melts the souls recently arrived.
The visit ends;
the man gives the Beast
a check with many zeros,
a handshake.

The elevator goes fast.
The cables run for hundreds of feet,
covered by the voices of elsewhere,
by the sudden tympanum
of Mozart's *Lacrimosa*
which fills the cabin.
Then, after the sound of pistons
of arcane gear,
the man arrives at his floor,
lifts the manhole,
and comes out.
Here, where money buys everything,
even a piece of five-star Hell
and a requiem that never ends.

Almost to the End

The hooker flips a switch
and turns on the lights of Eden—
red, purple, orange.
The road twists like a spine
trying to rid itself of too many quills,
then stretches and becomes infinite.

The waste on the roadside
looks like monuments—
statues of the moment—
remaining intact for only a few minutes
before being gnawed
by rats,
by winged insects,
by the lights of reality.

It's cold. January knows no half measures.
Eden is frozen.
The hooker is carved between tongues of ice.
You may confuse her
for a Renaissance fountain,
with small groups of heretic frogs at its feet
inflating their latex bodies.

Your car turns right,
as the sign says—

Eden is here—
pieces of flesh reflecting on the windows,
disappearing behind the last curve,
three hundred feet
of hedges of ribs, mosaics of tits,
and then you see her, your Eden,
the broken-down spaceship of your imagination,
towed by an old yellow truck
that slides
to the right and left.

Only the glue of your obsession
remains on the road,
mosquitoes trapped inside it,
and other hookers all around
asking too much money
for getting strangled,
almost to the end,
can't stay balanced
on the blade's edge.

The End?

75

Not if you come and take a look at Crystal Lake
Publishing's other titles.

www.crystallakepub.com/books

About the Author

Alessandro Manzetti is a horror, science fiction, weird fiction and dark poetry writer. His published work in Italian includes novels, long fiction, short story and dark poem collections, as well as many short stories that have appeared in anthologies. English publications include *The Massacre of the Mermaids*, *The Shaman and Other Shadows*, *Venus Intervention* with Corrine De Winter as co-author, *Dark Gates* with Paolo Di Orazio as co-author, and stories and poems that have appeared in both print and online USA and UK magazines and anthologies, such as Dark Moon Digest, The Horror Zine Magazine, Disturbed Digest, *Bones III* and others.

His poetry collection *Venus Intervention* was nominated for the Bram Stoker Awards 2014 and for the Elgin Award 2015, his poem *The Man Who Saw The World* was nominated for the Rhysling Awards 2015 and his poem *Interiora* was awarded with the Sinister Poetry Award 2014.

He can be found online at www.alessandromanzetti.net

Connect with the author:

Website: www.alessandromanzetti.net

Facebook: www.facebook.com/alessandro.manzetti.5

Twitter: www.twitter.com/amanzetti

Email: a.manzetti@hotmail.it

Connect with Crystal Lake Publishing

Website:
(and receive a free eBook by joining our newsletter)
www.crystallakepub.com
Facebook:
www.facebook.com/Crystallakepublishing
Twitter:
https://twitter.com/crystallakepub

With unmatched success over the last two years, Crystal Lake Publishing is quickly becoming the go-to press for Dark Fiction authors and fans. We publish the highest quality Dark Fiction books and poetry collections, which include Horror, Sci-Fi, Fantasy, Thrillers, Suspense, Supernatural, and Noir.

Crystal Lake Publishing puts integrity, honor and respect at the forefront of our operations.

We strive for each book and outreach program that's launched to not only entertain and touch or comment on issues that affect our readers, but also to strengthen and support the Dark Fiction field and its authors.

Not only do we publish authors who are legends in the field and as hardworking as us, but we look for men and women who care about their readers and fellow human beings. We only publish the very best Dark Fiction, and look forward to launching many new careers.

We strive to know each and every one of our readers, while building personal relationships with our authors, reviewers, bloggers, pod-casters, bookstores and libraries.

Crystal Lake Publishing is and will always be a beacon of what passion and dedication, combined with overwhelming teamwork and respect, can accomplish: Unique fiction you can't find anywhere else.

We do not just publish books, we present you worlds within your world, doors within your mind, from talented authors who sacrifice so much for a moment of your time.

This is what we believe in. What we stand for. This will be our legacy.

Welcome to Crystal Lake Publishing.

We hope you enjoyed this title. If so, we'd be grateful if you could leave a review on your blog or any of the other websites and outlets open to book reviews. Reviews are like gold to writers and publishers, since word-of-mouth is and will always be the best way to market a great book. And remember to keep an eye out for more of our books.

THANK YOU FOR PURCHASING THIS BOOK